About the Author

Chris Hall has served as a Royal Marine for twenty years and has completed multiple tours of Northern Ireland, Iraq and Afghanistan. Born in South London and educated at Dulwich College, he currently lives in Devon with his wife and three children and enjoys all outdoor and sporting pursuits, especially surfing, canoeing, rugby and cricket. He writes in his spare time and when travelling, and this is the first book he has written.

Chris Hall

PC Snap

and the

Case of the Escaped Lion

AUSTIN MACAULEY PUBLISHERS™
LONDON • CAMBRIDGE • NEW YORK • SHARJAH

A CIP catalogue record for this title is available from the British Library.

ISBN 9781787108615 (Paperback)
ISBN 9781787108622 (E-Book)

www.austinmacauley.com

First Published (2018)
Austin Macauley Publishers™ Ltd.
25 Canada Square
Canary Wharf
London
E14 5LQ

Dedication

Dedicated to my gorgeous JCC and three adorable little troublemakers.

Thanks for the idea, Dad.

CHAPTER 1

PC Snap woke with a start. A piercing ray of sunlight had naughtily crept under his window blind, tracked across his increasingly bright bedroom and straight into his bleary, recently-opened right eye. PC Snap's eye did not like this development and it rammed itself shut in a vain attempt to preserve the limited darkness of the night that was hanging on against the brightening morning. As if to brutally confirm to PC Snap that his favourite time of the day (night) was coming to an end, the shrill tone of his alarm clock forced both his eyes wide open again. PC Snap was committed to his sleep. He took pride in his ability to fall asleep anywhere, anytime and stay asleep anywhere, anytime. But the double whammy of light from the window and noise from the alarm added to that horrible internal feeling that he HAD to get up. So he opened his eyes this time for the last time, for today at least (unless he could find a quiet corner for thirty minutes after lunch!).

It might take PC Snap a while to wake up but once up, he was off. He had a clear routine to ensure that nothing was left out, much like his police work.

However, unlike most mornings, PC Snap's routine this morning began in a very different and painful fashion. To start his routine, PC Snap always leapt out of bed. Normally, this wasn't an issue. But this morning, PC Snap had forgotten about last night, when he had arrived back home late and had left his police uniform on the floor. As a result, PC Snap's usually safe leap out of bed ended up with one foot on his truncheon and the big toe of the other foot on his handcuffs. Neither was expected, or comfortable; in fact, both were unexpected and painful. We've all stubbed our toe or kicked something we shouldn't have, but not a truncheon or handcuffs. PC Snap grabbed both feet with his hands and squashed them hard to try and numb the throbbing pain. It only worked partially.

A shower, shave, hair brush and teeth clean followed in their usual order as well as a methodical iron of his police uniform. PC Snap took great pride in his uniform, with creases in his trousers and shirt, shiny boots and a brushed cap. No one was smarter than PC Snap, although many had tried. It was only as he made his way downstairs that PC Snap tried to work out why he had cleaned his teeth before breakfast. He did it most mornings and returned back upstairs after breakfast to clean them again.

Breakfast was important to PC Snap, very important! He prided himself on three things: his ability to sleep, his smart uniform and his eating prowess. A breakfast that didn't require a bowl, plate, knife, fork and spoon and didn't finish with a greasy frying pan that needed washing up wasn't a breakfast in his mind. PC Snap knew it wasn't healthy for him, but it was easy and deeply satisfying. Why? Because PC Snap lived with his mum.

PC Snap's mum was exactly what everyone wanted their mother to be. She was proud of him, but firm. She helped him but didn't mother him. She was generally right and if he didn't think she was, then he would have a think about it and it usually turned out that she was. And to top it off, she was a dangerously good cook, especially of PC Snap's favourite foods.

This morning's breakfast wasn't that big, mainly because having finished work late last night, PC Snap's traditional end-of-day snack, a slice of ginger cake and a cup of cocoa, was still wallowing inside him. That being said, the breakfast wasn't small either; two sausages, two rashes of bacon, two hash browns, toast, tea and orange juice. Once he had finished his breakfast, PC Snap grabbed a second cup of tea and sat in his favourite comfy chair, which for some reason only had one arm and no one could remember where it had come from.

The main reason for this second cup of tea was that it allowed PC Snap
to spend more time with his beloved best friend Louie, a gorgeous black
Labrador with smooth, sleek hair, made smoother and sleeker by years
of stroking, patting and grooming. PC Snap wondered if Louie was the
smoothest dog in the world. But, the most stunning part of Louie were his eyes.
Two black lumps of coal taken from the darkest corner of the deepest mine;
they were a kaleidoscope of love, wisdom and unmitigated affection. Slumped
in his bed in the corner of the living room by the log burner, with his chin on his
paws and with his lips hanging slightly unevenly in a way that made him look
like he was smiling, Louie owned PC Snap's heart.

PC Snap got up from his chair in the same manner he had for many years. He
ran his calloused hand over Louie's smooth head and uttered Louie's favourite
words, "Come on then, boy!"

The speed with which Louie went from lying down and completely relaxed to
four-legged rocket always amazed PC Snap. Once those words had been
uttered each morning, Louie was like a bullet from a gun. He seemed to rise
up, turn around 180 degrees in mid-air and be halfway to the door before PC
Snap had finished the sentence. PC Snap had seen a lot of people try and

run fast from a standing start, mainly criminals, but none of them had a patch on Louie. However, as happened most mornings, halfway to the door Louie realised the need to stop and remembered that his brakes were not what they once were, which meant they should have been applied a few steps earlier. The inside of the door made an effective crash barrier, but fortunately, Louie's head didn't seem to be affected too much by the impact.

Before he left the house each morning to head to work, PC Snap made sure that he had everything he needed; truncheon, whistle, handcuffs, notebook, pencil and of course, Louie. Yes, Louie is a police dog, and a very good one at that. Ever since PC Snap had rescued him from a burning building, Louie has been his partner. PC Snap used to keep track of how many patrols they had been on, how many criminals they had arrested, how many lives they had saved, but there were now simply too many to count. PC Snap had, however, managed to keep track of the bravery awards Louie had been awarded; three, more than any other police dog in Devon. They were a very effective team and the best of friends.

With all the tools of his trade on hand, PC Snap opened the front door, called over his shoulder a "goodbye" to his mum and stepped out of the door.

At least he tried to, because blocking his way, as they were most days of the school holidays, were Beth and Archie, the two kids from next door. The barrage of questions was relentless.

"Who are you going to arrest today, PC Snap?" "Who did you arrest yesterday?" "Who will you arrest tomorrow?" "Can we stroke Louie?" "Can we try the handcuffs on?" "Can we come to work with you?"

PC Snap did his best to deal with each question in turn but, before he could answer the first one, he was being asked the second and usually the third! As much as they made getting to work harder, PC Snap loved Archie and Beth and they loved him too, but not as much as they loved Louie, and Louie knew it. The poor animal could barely move under the pats and strokes Beth and Archie lavished him with. He adored every one of them, returning them in kind with licks, woofs and tail wags.

Aside from a four-inch height gap between them, Beth and Archie could have been twins. Beth was thirteen months older than Archie and, as she loved to say, that meant she was in charge. She advertised herself as a tomboy, which to an extent she was, but she was a beautiful, chubby cheeked, strong-willed little girl with a smile to die for, beautiful, long loosely-curled light-brown hair with streaks of blonde in it that increased in number, length and thickness as the summer unfolded. Beth rated herself as something of a detective, having read numerous Secret Seven, Famous Five, Scooby Doo and Harry Potter books. She was a bit of a George, Anne, Daphne and Hermione rolled into one. On more than one occasion, she had helped PC Snap unpick a mystery and, although PC Snap never told her, she was a born detective.

Her little (although PC Snap never said that to him) brother Archie was very different. He was a six-year-old boy through and through, from the ripped baseball cap on his head all the way down past his snotty face, food-stained T Shirt, dirty shorts, odd socks and well-worn trainers. Everything about Archie screamed 'urchin', and to an extent he was, but inside was a heart so warm it pulsated affection and love, especially where Louie was concerned. On many a night, Archie had fallen asleep on Louie in front of the log fire and had to be carried home by PC Snap and gently lowered into bed without washing a face that need a good scrub, or brushing hair that would take a rake and a prayer in the morning to get it in good order. PC Snap saw in Archie much of himself when he was younger, and many times Archie had proved himself to be brave and courageous, and not a little intelligent.

Although clearly not officially police officers, PC Snap had long ago given Beth and Archie unofficial police numbers. They had even been given them in an official ceremony at the Police Station. Beth was PCO29 and Archie was PC251 and whenever they were assisting PC Snap, or just playing cops and robbers in the garden, they would proudly wear the insignia. Every now and then, PC Snap would hold a 'Snap' inspection to check that they had polished their badges. They always had, and their mother had told him that without fail, they would clean them every night, often sleeping in them, just in case PC Snap should wake them in the middle of the night, needing their assistance. PC Snap was keen to ensure that Beth and Archie knew when they could help and when they couldn't, and they understood that some things just needed to be done by adults.

This morning was one of those adult mornings and much to their frustration, PC Snap had to tell Beth and Archie that they couldn't come to work with him. Noting the anguished look on their faces, and Louie's, PC Snap agreed that they could bring his lunch down to the station when it was ready. With that, PC Snap and Louie, who was glued to his heel, set off down Staddon Hill and into town.

Heybrook Thomas was PC Snap's home town and was nestled on either side of the River Bovvy and next to the coast. Built on fishing and tourism, it was the kind of town that most people dreamt of growing up in. With steep banks rising up on both sides, PC Snap had felt when he was a child that the majority of the houses he knew and loved might fall into the river at any time. The tightly packed cottages, some with gorgeous thatched rooves that PC Snap adored, were interwoven with some newer houses, shops, markets, the harbour, a train station and all the other buildings one would expect in a bustling town.

Unless you knew it was there, you could easily miss the Police Station. It was an old school house and, apart from the blue flowers outside and a notice board in front of it, there was little to distinguish it in any way. The sign above the door, which read 'Police Station', was well worn and in desperate need of repair. But there was no rush, like most things in Heybrook Thomas, it would happen in time.

It didn't take PC Snap and Louie long, having escaped from the barrage of Archie and Beth's questions, to reach the Police Station. Long enough to give Louie a decent leg stretch and a chance to do what dogs need to do in morning, but no more. PC Snap wasn't worried as Louie always finished each day utterly exhausted.

There were only three people who worked at the station; PC Snap, Sgt Brown and Police Community Support Officer Lucy Tucker. Sgt Brown was exactly what a Police Sgt should be; very tall, with broad shoulders, an immaculate bearing and appearance and a manner that would calm the most fraught and tense situation. PC Snap wasn't sure if Sgt Brown could actually put his hands in front of his body, as they were always resting on his lower back, one placed precisely over the other. PC Snap had long ago assumed that Sgt Brown had something wrong with his feet, or his boots, because he never stood still. He was always slowly rocking from heel to toe and back again in an almost hypnotic fashion that PC Snap found very reassuring. Sgt Brown never raised his voice, he didn't need to, because wherever he was,

everyone else was quiet.

PCSO Lucy Tucker, however, was very, very different. PC Snap had never seen lightning up close, thankfully, but he imagined Lucy's hair to be the same colour. It was so brightly blonde and straight that PC Snap often wondered whether it was real. The only thing that could distract you from Lucy's hair

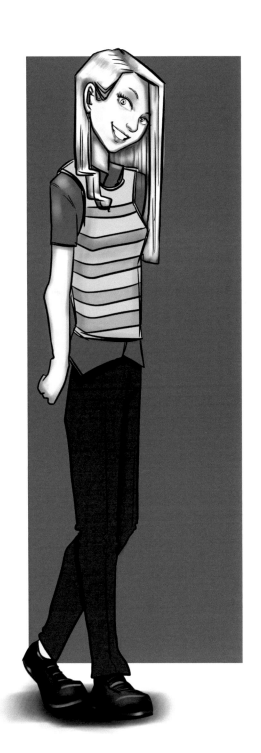

were her eyes. Two luminescent balls of cornflower blue, or at least PC Snap thought they were, for Lucy had never stood still long enough for him to be completely sure. The first prisoner she had arrested described Lucy as like a firework in a bean tin and he wasn't wrong! Where she got her energy from, no one knew, but there was an awful lot of it!

CHAPTER 2

"So what's on the cards today?" shouted Lucy with an energetic burst akin to the lid being blown off the top of a fizzy pop drink. Louie raised an expectant eyebrow and PC Snap waited optimistically to see what the day might offer.

"The circus," replied Sgt Brown in his usual understated and methodical manner.

"The circus?" replied Lucy in a puzzled and mildly disappointed manner.

"Yes," came the terse reply. "It's in town and we need to look after it."

"How much looking after does a circus need?" replied Lucy, coming across as more than a little frustrated.

"Who knows?" replied Sgt Brown, "But probably more than you might think. It opens at ten, so you need to leave now if you want to get there on time. Off you go!"

As PC Snap left the station with Louie and Lucy, he knew what was coming, 'disappointment management'. Lucy wanted excitement, lots of it, and more tomorrow, more the day after and double the day after that, and keep it coming! PC Snap admired her energy and drive, but Lucy needed a big city to give her what she wanted and Heybrook Thomas wasn't a big city. It had its

fair share of incidents, but not on the scale that Lucy wanted or needed. So the journey to the park was spent trying to placate Lucy and reassure her that she wasn't missing out. He repeatedly made the point that she didn't know what was around the corner and she should be careful what she wished for. PC Snap had had this chat with Lucy many times so his speech was well-rehearsed. Lucy would hear but not always listen, and who could blame her? But even Lucy couldn't hide her excitement when they arrived at the park. The circus was enormous, far bigger than last year, with everything you would expect and more. There was a big top, lions, jugglers, clowns, elephants, fairground rides, burger stands, candy floss, a coconut shy and much, much more. The crowds were already gathering in expectation of the gates opening and, before they knew it, PC Snap and Lucy were organising the crowds and dealing with all the things that happen when lots of people are together. People were pushing in, children were getting lost, things were getting lost and dozens and dozens of people wanted to stroke Louie. Louie had an amazing ability to calm people down, which was a good thing as the gates were late opening. Unfortunately, several mums and dads were getting very frustrated and lots of children were getting very bored and mischievous.

But, eventually, the gates did open and the crowds surged in and before you knew it, every ride was whirling, spinning, rising, diving and looping, accompanied by an endless cacophony of screams, shrieks and whoops of delight. PC Snap, Lucy and Louie spent an enjoyable yet busy day dealing with a myriad of problems from lost children to jelly babies that were stuck up noses. PC Snap was delighted when his usual lunch of a homemade pasty was delivered by an excited Beth and Archie. who had come to the circus for the afternoon. Obviously, they had brought Louie some treats as well and these were gratefully gobbled up by the greedy mutt.

It wasn't until later on in the day that PC Snap realised that they hadn't been into the big top to see the actual circus show itself. So just before the four p.m. show started, PC Snap, Lucy and Louie sneaked into the back of the tent to watch. PC Snap had always admired the skill and bravery of circus performers. As a young child, he remembered watching in awe the trapeze-artists and lion-tamers and, despite being an adult, that awe hadn't left him. The show was mesmerising, death-defying and hilarious. PC Snap loved every minute of it. From the clowns with their massive feet and red noses to the acrobats and jugglers, the crowd was in raptures throughout.

The show culminated with the lion-tamers, perhaps PC Snap's favourite part. There were three lions, two females called Sandy and Margaret and a male called Paul, whose mane shuddered and shimmered with every step he took. PC Snap had no idea how you would begin to train a lion, but he loved the outcome regardless, as did the crowd. The show ended with one of the lion-tamers, Cynthia, placing her head inside Paul's mouth, accompanied by loud cheers and applause from the audience, followed by shouts of 'encore!', 'encore!' Despite the fake protestation of the tamers, everyone knew there would be one more trick. However, no one expected Cynthia to ask for a volunteer.

"I need someone who is calm, brave and courageous!" Cynthia shouted out across the ring to the audience. No one moved. Everyone wondered what the volunteer would be required to do and until they knew, no one was going to put their hand up. Cynthia asked again, but was greeted by a rather prolonged, awkward silence.

"PC Snap will do it!" shrieked a young voice, breaking the silence and making a few people jump in their seats. Everyone in the crowd looked round to see where the voice had come from. "PC Snap will do it!" repeated the same voice. PC Snap checked his lips, but he was fairly sure that they weren't

moving. Whilst checking his lips again, the same voice echœd out around the tent, "PC Snap will do it!" This time most of the eyes of the crowd, including PC Snap's, settled on the far corner of the tent where a young boy with a dirty face sat next to a girl with blonde streaks in her loosely curled hair. The boy's lips moved again, "PC Snap will do it!" PC Snap recoiled in horror as he realised that it was none other than Archie, sitting next to Beth, who was doing all the shouting. However, Archie was struggling to shout because spread across his face was the widest, impish, most mischievous grin you could imagine. "Why you little..." whispered PC Snap under his breath.

But before he could finish his sentence, Cynthia had grasped Archie's offer and confidently announced to the crowd, "PC Snap, we have a volunteer!" PC Snap's mouth went dry, he started to sweat and his legs nearly buckled under him. He felt as though he was having an out-of-body experience as without apparently doing anything, he found himself moving to the edge of the ring, climbing over the barrier and shaking Cynthia's hand. Throughout, all he could see was Archie's ever-broadening grin.

"Thank you for volunteering," said Cynthia to PC Snap.

"I didn't," he replied.

Cynthia ignored PC Snap and turned to the crowd, asking for a huge round of applause for the brave PC Snap. The crowd went wild. To make it even worse, Cynthia asked the crowd what PC Snap should do! PC Snap couldn't believe it, what on earth was she doing?

Having played to the crowd by repeatedly asking them for ideas, Cynthia bought them all to a hushed silence. It took a while, as by this stage they were very, very excited and almost out of control. "I've got it!" she cried, raising her hands in the air in a state of excitement. She lowered her fingers to her lips to hush the crowd. "PC Snap", announced Cynthia, "will place his head," and then she paused for effect, "in Paul's mouth!"

The crowd went nuts. The noise was so loud that had PC Snap not been worried about his legs giving way, he would have worried about the tent collapsing. After several requests from Cynthia, the noise fell to a manageable level. Cynthia took PC Snap over to where Paul was prowling in his cage. She whispered to PC Snap what was going to happen. "I'll put him on his platform and open his mouth, then you put your head in, take it out and walk away. Simple as that."

Simple as that, thought PC Snap, *simple as that!* Lost in a world of his own concerns, PC Snap barely heard Cynthia explain the plan to the crowd. Again, the crowd roared and cheered and it took Cynthia some time to calm them down (although PC Snap didn't think she was trying too hard).

Cynthia made her way over to him again, placing a hand on his shaking shoulder. She whispered, "Don't worry, it will be fine, it's only gone wrong twice in twenty years." PC Snap thought he might be sick. The tent appeared to be spinning and amongst the laughing faces, PC Snap could just make out a worried-looking Lucy and a large smirk over most of Archie's face. Beth looked as concerned as PC Snap felt.

Striking a somewhat more serious tone, Cynthia turned to the crowd and ordered them to be quiet until PC Snap had removed his head from Paul's jaws. The crowd instantly obeyed and a hush descended.

The out-of-body experience that PC Snap had felt when he entered the ring returned with a vengeance. The words that Cynthia was saying to him barely registered. He felt as if he were gliding towards Paul's mouth without moving his feet. This close, Paul was enormous. PC Snap couldn't remember a time when he had been this scared. He vaguely registered Paul jumping onto his platform and sitting down on his hind legs. Cynthia said something and Paul's

mouth opened to reveal two rows of humungous, sharp, shiny teeth; so many that PC Snap couldn't count them all. Somehow, PC Snap felt his head moving towards this nightmare picture. He couldn't stop himself, however hard he tried. PC Snap's world had been reduced to a mass of teeth, a big black hole and the sound of his pulse in his head, thudding, banging like a huge bass drum being beaten by an enormous man, with an enormous stick.

And then silence. The feeling was very bizarre and although PC Snap could see the lights of the tent, his world had become dark and very smelly. The inside of Paul's mouth was very, very smelly. It stank! In fact, it stank so much that PC Snap thought that he might be sick.

PC Snap found himself looking around. He had his head in a lion's mouth and was actually looking around! He noticed that his teeth weren't that clean close up. Paul's tongue was very red and covered in veins and inside his mouth, it was bizarrely warm.

At last, PC Snap felt himself withdrawing from the mouth. The smell and heat reduced in strength and the lights became brighter and brighter. And then, from nowhere, a tidal wave of noise descended on him as the crowd went wild. Cynthia grabbed him on both shoulders, babbling words that PC Snap couldn't really hear, but she seemed to be asking why had he stayed in there so long and why had he gone in so far? She appeared to be smiling, but PC Snap wasn't sure. As his senses returned to him, he managed a wave to the crowd and even gave a poor excuse for a bow.

Eventually, the applause and cheering began to ease and the crowd made for the exits with the children excitedly chatting to each other about PC Snap and the adults exchanging comments such as, "He's a lunatic," "Why did he stay in that long?" and "You wouldn't catch me doing that."

Cynthia grabbed PC Snap and took him towards the stage door. She seemed as excited as the crowd. She repeatedly said, "We have never had a show like that before, you were amazing, you're a natural!" and other such comments. From nowhere a clown with smudged face-paint and a crooked bow tie thrust a cup of tea into PC Snap's hand with the comment, "You're a lunatic!" before walking off. As PC Snap took a sip, he felt a thud on his left leg and then a thud on his right, which made him spill his tea and slightly burn his lip. He looked down to see Beth clamped to one leg and Archie to the other.

"You were amazing, you were so brave, I didn't think you would do it!" they both repeated together until PC Snap managed to prise them off his legs one by one using only one hand whilst trying not to spill his tea, again.

Eventually, he found a seat and as he sat down, he felt the energy leave his body in one huge wave. Suddenly, he was exhausted, completely and utterly drained. He felt as though he couldn't lift a finger or move the smallest muscle in his body, even if his life depended on it.

At some point, Lucy and Louie arrived. Both were looking extremely concerned. Louie wedged his head between PC Snap's legs and fixed him with his most intense stare. Lucy kept saying how pale he looked and how he needed to lie down and raise his feet and eat something and have a sleep and unbutton the top of his shirt. PC Snap wasn't sure how he could do all those things at the same time, but he tried to comply with the multiple instructions. Having tried his best to sleep, eat, drink and unbutton his tunic at the same time, PC Snap gave up, stood up, and announced to the assembled throng that he was OK. He was greeted by a barrage of replies to the contrary, but PC Snap carried on trying to leave the tent with a dog between his legs, a child attached to each leg and a PCSO trying to force him to sit down. In desperation, he opened a door that he thought might lead him out of the tent, only to find himself face to face with Cynthia.

"Thank you for volunteering today," she said.

"It was my pleasure," he lied as their hands shook for slightly longer than normal. There was an awkward pause, which made everyone else in the room feel uncomfortable, until Cynthia asked, "I suppose you're trying to find your way out?"

"Yes," said PC Snap, slightly cautiously as now he wasn't sure he wanted to leave. "This way then," she said as she lightly brushed past him out of the door he had entered and turned left.

The entourage of people, children and dog that were gathered around PC Snap obligingly followed him out and then along a canvas tunnel through many twists and turns until they reached fresh air and so much sunlight that PC Snap had trouble seeing for a moment or two.

"Here you go, normality," said Cynthia as she turned towards PC Snap. She extended her hand again and PC Snap realised how striking her face was. "Maybe I'll see you again soon," she said, disappearing back into the tent before PC Snap could reply.

Back in the outdoors, PC Snap's senses quickly returned to him, as did most of the crowd who had been in the tent. They descended on him in such numbers that PC Snap was worried about the safety of the smaller children.

However, the atmosphere was one of excitement as PC Snap was again swamped by a deluge of questions and comments. One by one, the crowd slowly dispersed until eventually only PC Snap, Lucy and Louie were left. Archie and Beth had disappeared with the others, which was a good thing for Archie, as PC Snap wouldn't have minded a little word in the troublemaker's ear. PC Snap, Lucy and Louie headed for the main entrance.

"So how was it?" Lucy asked.

"Bit smelly," replied PC Snap to a quizzical look from Lucy and a tilt of the head from Louie. "And dark," added PC Snap, "but mostly smelly."

CHAPTER 3

PC Snap called Sgt Brown on his radio. Sgt Brown was well aware of what had happened at the fair, although the way the radio affected his voice, PC Snap wasn't sure if he was amused, annoyed or bewildered. Either way, he was happy for PC Snap and Lucy to head directly home, saying that he would lock up the station and see them in the morning.

PC Snap and Lucy said goodbye at the old Post Office. Lucy gave Louie an affectionate pat on his head, and PC Snap and Louie headed up the hill towards home. There was no sign of Archie and Beth as PC Snap passed their house, and he assumed they were either in bed or in trouble. Either way, although he loved them, he was glad they weren't there as he couldn't face another load of questions about his experience. Besides, a slight drizzle had started to fall and PC Snap was getting just a little damp. However, his over-riding feeling was one of hunger, and he knew tea would be waiting for him. PC Snap slipped his key in the door and as always, Louie tried, and somehow succeeded, to get in the door before it was really wide enough for him reasonably to do so. With his claws tink tinking on the tiles, he hurtled towards the kitchen where he knew PC Snap's mum, and more importantly his tea, would be waiting. Both were, as always, and what quickly followed was their evening ritual of stroking and eating, followed by Louie collapsing in his bed by the log fire and instantly going to sleep, jaw on paws as always. PC Snap, as he was every evening, was ignored until this nightly ritual had finished.

He didn't mind this because he knew that some form of delicious tea would be waiting for him as well. Tonight was no exception. Homemade bread and butter to start, toad in the hole with crispy potato wedges and squeaky beans and then apple crumble and custard to finish. Perfect! PC Snap's mum knew very well that for her son, eating was a serious business. He always ate at a pace that suggested he thought that at any time, someone might appear from nowhere and steal his food. Whilst she was delighted that he devoured her food so readily, she did worry about the long-term health consequences. When it came to meals, the only thing PC Snap worried about was if there were seconds. He needn't have worried, there were always plenty!

After dinner, PC Snap collapsed in the one-armed armchair and contemplated the world, knowing that in turn Louie was contemplating him.

After tea, PC Snap's evenings were divided into two groups. Those evenings when Louie would pad over and slump onto PC Snap's feet so that he couldn't move, or clamber onto his lap so that he couldn't move; either way he was stuck in his chair. The other group of evenings were when Louie couldn't or wouldn't leave his bed. Tonight was the former and PC Snap helped Louie onto his lap and sighed as the warmth of his beloved dog seeped into him. Both were soon fast asleep, dreaming separate dreams and occasionally stirring or twitching.

Along with the speed with which PC Snap ate his food, the other thing about PC Snap that never ceased to surprise his mother, was the speed with which he was hungry again. Tonight was no exception. Having been slumbering in his chair for an hour, PC Snap optimistically called through to the kitchen for any left overs. His mum knew what this meant and appeared a few minutes later with his usual pre-bedtime snack; a slice of ginger cake and a cup of hot cocoa, with a small treat for Louie, who affectionately slobbered on her hand as she popped it into his mouth. In between bites of cake and sips of hot chocolate, PC Snap's mother managed to establish what had happened at the circus before both PC Snap and Louie nodded off again. Knowing this was the last coherent response she would get from either of them that evening, she went upstairs to bed. The only acknowledgement she received was a raised eye lid from Louie and a slight twitch from PC Snap. She didn't mind; she normally got a lot less.

It was normally Louie's need for a wee that dictated when PC Snap went to bed. If Louie jumping off PC Snap's lap to head to the back door didn't wake him, then his tapping on the door to be let out would. PC Snap would dutifully let him out and back in again, before they would both climb the stairs for their pre-bed rituals before they fell asleep. It didn't take long.

PC Snap slept the sleep of the dead, so it took a lot to wake him. Tonight 'a lot' was Sgt Brown shouting into the police radio for him to wake up. PC Snap had been dreaming that Paul the lion had put his head in PC Snap's mouth when he awoke with a start. Louie did his best to ignore the commotion, but it still woke him up.

"Sgt Brown, this is PC Snap. Send your message, over," PC Snap muttered into the radio. The radio squawked in response a long message about failing to wake up and turn the volume up and how deep can a man sleep and get yourself to the station as a lion has escaped! PC Snap sat bolt upright in bed.

A lion has escaped? Even Louie was awake now. When he needed to, PC Snap could wake up pretty quickly and tonight was one of those moments. He dressed as quickly as he could and tiptœd downstairs. He always tried to leave the house quietly when he got a call in the middle of the night, but he was usually undone by Louie who, in his excitement, would descend the stairs so quickly that he would usually end up falling down them, landing in a heap at the bottom and sometimes taking PC Snap down with him. PC Snap's attempts to calm Louie only made him more excited, until the best thing to do was to just get him out of the house. Tonight was worse than normal and PC Snap couldn't believe the whole street wasn't awake by the time he closed the front door!

The first thing PC Snap noticed was that it was dark, really dark. No stars, no moon, no light. He checked he had everything he needed; whistle, truncheon, notebook, pencil and handcuffs, and when he was content he had, he opened the garden gate to leave. As he lifted the latch with a slight squeak, he jumped with surprise when a little voice said, "So where are you off to then?"

This was quickly followed by another voice saying, "Please tell us, please?"

"What are you two doing up?" PC Snap said to Beth and Archie – as it couldn't be anyone else.

"We heard your radio through the wall of our bedroom saying that a lion has escaped, so we've come to help."

PC Snap cursed himself for having the volume on his radio so high and told them both to go back inside.

"Can't," said Archie.

"What do you mean 'can't'?" replied PC Snap.

"We haven't got a key and the door is closed, so we're locked out."

"Can we come with you?"

"No."

"But we must!"

"Why?"

"Because you can't wake mum up and you can't leave us here when a lion is on the loose."

PC Snap paused. He didn't want to wake their mum up, but he also didn't want to take them to the station and he couldn't leave them where they were. A cacophony of "pleases" made his mind up.

"Quiet you two or you'll wake the whole street," he hushed. "Come on then," he said as he strode off down the street. Both children squealed with delight and excitement as they ran after PC Snap and Louie.

None of them noticed the kitchen lights flickering on in both houses. Both mothers knew what was happening and both knew that in a few hours their respective off–spring would return, excited but tired and needing food; food that wouldn't make itself.

CHAPTER 4

Beth and Archie struggled to keep up with PC Snap and Louie, but they managed it, just, whilst asking never-ending questions. What are we doing? Where's the lion? Which lion has escaped? Are you scared? Where's Lucy? Is your truncheon heavy? You've forgotten your handcuffs etc, etc. PC Snap ignored them all and walked even faster, taking care to make sure he didn't tread on Louie and wasn't tripped over by Beth and Archie in their excitement as they tried to run between his legs. In comparison to getting to the station, looking for a lion was going to be easy.

By the time they arrived at the station, the building was awash with lights and full to the brim with people talking excitedly. There must have been at least twenty people in the station and even the commanding presence of Sgt Brown was not restoring order the way it usually did. Lucy was doing her best, but nothing was working. The arrival of PC Snap, Louie, Beth and Archie didn't help. Louie received his usual affectionate welcome and Beth and Archie were greeted with surprise and a little horror that they were up at this time of the

night. PC Snap did his best to explain, but eventually gave up.

Fighting through the crowd to Sgt Brown's office, PC Snap plonked Archie and Beth on a chair and told them not to move until he told them they could. Eventually, he managed to close the door to the office but not before Cynthia had, much to PC Snap's surprise and delight, snuck in.

Sgt Brown did what he always did and briefed a very clear plan. He had divided the town into sections, which each person in the station would search. If they found Paul, they were to call the station and Cynthia would come to secure him. PC Snap and Cynthia would search the park as this is where Sgt Brown thought Paul would most likely have gone.

Once Sgt Brown had finished explaining his plan, PC Snap and Lucy went out into the foyer and tried to explain what everyone needed to do. Somehow, the station slowly cleared with PC Snap, Louie and Cynthia the last to leave. PC Snap couldn't see Beth and Archie, but he assumed that they were still in Sgt Brown's office, as he had told them to be.

Once PC Snap and Cynthia had turned the corner, the lights of the Police Station disappeared into the darkness and quiet descended once again.

"How did he escape?" PC Snap whispered.

"We don't know," Cynthia whispered back, "but we need to find him. If he doesn't eat soon, he will be very hungry, and that means trouble for us all." They both paused to think what that might mean and then put it to the back of their minds. At the front of PC Snap's mind was the image of Paul's teeth; big, shiny and sharp. It was not a pleasant thought.

PC Snap and Cynthia exchanged pleasantries but nothing more as they briskly walked to the park. When they arrived, the gates were locked shut but with impressive gymnastic ability Cynthia sprang over the head-high metal fence with ease. In a slightly less athletic fashion, PC Snap followed her, landing awkwardly at her feet. Luckily, it was very dark, so Cynthia couldn't see the embarrassment on his face.

The two of them set off into the increasing gloom and both felt slightly chilly as the dew began to fall, making them rather damp. They tiptoed through the undergrowth for what seemed like hours. PC Snap was not surprised to hear his stomach rumble after a while, but he was surprised at how long the rumble went on for and how loud it was. When it rumbled for the second time, but even longer and louder than the first, PC Snap began to think something was wrong with him. Cynthia grabbed his arm and whispered,

"Did you hear that?"

"Sorry, it's my stomach."

"What?" queried Cynthia.

"That rumbling nose, it's my stomach."

"No not that, I think I can hear Paul purring, he's very close."

PC Snap realised his error and was again grateful that the darkness hid his increasingly red cheeks.

They emerged into a small clearing in the undergrowth where the mist seemed even thicker. The purring, if that's what it was, was getting louder and louder, but the mist prevented them from seeing anything. To PC Snap's surprise, Cynthia started whispering "Paul, Paul," as if she were calling for Tiddles the cat. Her first calls were surprisingly answered by two high-pitched panicking voices whispering very slowly, "PC Snap, help us!" The second time PC Snap heard this, he knew who it was. He couldn't work out where they were, but he knew who they were, and that was not a good thing. How Beth and Archie had got into the park could be worked out later, but for now, PC Snap couldn't see anything, but he knew that Beth, Archie and Paul were all nearby and that wasn't good. In fact, it was very bad; very bad indeed.

What happened next came as something of a surprise to PC Snap. He didn't see Cynthia fall but he heard the thud as she hit the floor. He guessed she had tripped over something and banged her head but either way, she wasn't moving. PC Snap reached down to see if she was still breathing. She was, but she had definitely knocked herself out and PC Snap could see a small trickle of blood coming from her head.

At this point, the mist lifted slightly and PC Snap could see around the clearing. This should have been a good thing, but it wasn't. For in the corner of the clearing he could see a very scared Beth and Archie hugging each other only a matter of feet in front of Paul.

A snarling Paul saw PC Snap as PC Snap saw the snarling Paul. If this wasn't a big enough issue, PC Snap suddenly realised why Paul was snarling. PC Snap was kneeling over Paul's beloved trainer, who to all intents and purposes appeared to be dead, with blood coming out of her head. Paul's snarl grew at the same intensity as PC Snap's feeling of total panic.

CHAPTER 5

It took a lot to scare PC Snap, really scare him. The sort of scared that pumps adrenalin around your body and leaves you feeling either paralysed or invigorated. PC Snap had been in many, many dangerous situations. He was used to them, to an extent, but they generally involved people and PC Snap understood people. He knew how to deal with them and talk to them and was fairly good at it. He wasn't used to lions, didn't understand them and definitely couldn't talk to them. He certainly wasn't used to angry lions that think that you have just killed the one person in the world they love and trust. He also wasn't used to lions that were very close to small children for whom he cared deeply.

In the words of Sgt Brown, this was "a bit of a situation", and that was putting it mildly. PC Snap suddenly noticed a rapidly repetitive thudding noise. A thudding noise that had broken the silence that was, until recently, completely encompassing. It took PC Snap a while to work out what it was. It was him. It was the sound of his heart thudding in his chest. This unnerved PC Snap, and he felt even worse when he realised that he was now profusely sweating and his throat was bone dry.

He was shaken from his trance-like state by two very scared voices whispering very quietly, "PC Snap, what do we do?" PC Snap turned towards Beth and Archie and saw in their eyes what they probably saw in his... pure fear. Time appeared to have slowed and what PC Snap thought was taking forever was actually only a few seconds. But PC Snap was lost, he had no idea what to do, which was very unusual for him, if not completely unique, and he didn't like it. PC Snap had absolutely no idea what to do.

In the midst of his paralysing fear, PC Snap had completely forgotten about Louie until he caught sight of a blur in the periphery of his vision. As he rotated his head towards the blur, what slowly came into focus was the slightly bizarre sight of Louie rolling around in the grass like dogs do when they are trying to scratch their back, but can't. It was as if Louie had no idea of the peril they were in but instead, was having a lovely time giving himself a back scratch on a fir cone or some such item on the ground.

Quickly glancing back at Paul, PC Snap realised that not only had Paul noticed this unexpected activity but he was as bemused by it as PC Snap was. The lion tilted his enormous maned head slightly to one side and, maybe PC

Snap imagined this, but it appeared that Paul had turned up the corner of his mouth and was grinning, even smiling.

If this turn of events had relaxed the situation somewhat, it didn't last long as Paul leapt over to the wriggling Louie who, to all intents and purposes, seemed to be oblivious to the lion's presence.

Simultaneously, PC Snap, Beth and Archie took a sharp intake of breath. Beth closed her eyes and, although they didn't know it, all three of them were thinking the same thing. All three of them were waiting for the sickening crunch of teeth on bone as Paul ripped Louie apart as if he were nothing but a rag doll. Beth even let out a shriek of terror, which she stifled herself by throwing her hand across her mouth.

But the crunch of teeth on bone, the howls of pain and tearing noise of ripping flesh and muscle never came. To the disbelief of all three of them, Paul began to sniff Louie as any dog would another dog. It was an utterly incredible sight. A ferocious, enormous, half-tonne lion sniffing a smooth black Labrador, who by this stage was lying on his back with his paws raised and the wonderful look on his face which dogs have which screams,

"Play with me, pleeaassee!!!"

And that is just what Paul did. The two of them played, lightly cuffing each other with paws, playfully trying to lock their jaws on each other's limbs, yapping at each other, at least in Louie's case, and having a game of rough and tumble wrestling as if they were two newly born pups.

PC Snap had no idea whether Louie knew what he was doing or not. Had he leapt into the situation because he realised PC Snap didn't know what to do, or because he had an itchy back, or because he wanted to play with what he thought was just a big dog with a funny haircut? Either way, it worked. PC Snap even found himself smiling a little and as he looked at Beth and Archie, he could see that they were actually giggling at this playful and innocent scene. As the two new friends continued to wrestle and roll around, PC Snap realised they still weren't out of danger. Paul was still Paul, Beth and Archie were still in a life-threatening situation, as was he, and Cynthia was still lying at his feet unconscious and bleeding. He looked down to see how she was doing only to realise that she was no longer where she had been. He began to look round to see where she had gone, when he heard a controlling voice behind him say, "Don't move a muscle." PC Snap was used to taking orders, so he didn't move. He assumed the instruction was from Cynthia, but it had been delivered in

such a forceful manner that he half expected it to be Sgt Brown.

What followed seemed like a never-ending pause, but probably only lasted a few seconds, but in that time PC Snap saw Beth and Archie's faces turn from ones of laughter to ones of complete horror. Before he had time to think why, there was a very loud pop from behind him and thud from in front of him. Something appeared in the glorious golden side of Paul that looked like a small dart. Paul quizzically looked at the dart before licking his lips and then falling over, almost squashing Louie, who had just as little an idea as to what was going on as Paul.

Beth screamed in a way that only young girls can, "She's killed him, she's killed him!" and promptly collapsed on the floor, sobbing big, fat tears.

Cynthia rapidly appeared from behind PC Snap and ran towards Paul, carrying what looked like a gun. PC Snap took a sharp breath, unclear as to what had happened but instinctively thinking that all was not well. Cynthia knelt beside Paul for a matter of seconds before running over to Beth and holding her tightly, repeatedly saying, "It's a tranquiliser gun, it's a tranquiliser gun. I haven't killed him, he's going to be okay!"

CHAPTER 6

As the circus truck pulled out of the park which was now dimly lit by the rising sun, PC Snap slumped on a bench and took stock. It seemed that the playful noise of Paul and Louie wrestling had woken Cynthia from her unconscious state. As PC Snap, Beth and Archie had been focussing on Paul and Louie, they hadn't noticed Cynthia gather herself, prepare the tranquiliser gun and get ready to fire. Just as she was ready and could hit Paul without hitting Louie, PC Snap had begun to turn around, hence her very direct command to him to stand still. Trying to hit a moving lion without hitting a moving dog was hard enough, without the added problem of trying to avoid hitting a moving policeman.

From Beth and Archie's perspective, Cynthia was going to shoot and kill Paul, hence Beth's scream of anguish. But unintentionally, Beth's scream had caused Paul and Louie to stand still, giving Cynthia the perfect chance to shoot. PC Snap knew that the dart hadn't caused Paul any pain and, luckily, he was asleep almost instantly. Cynthia had quickly calmed Beth down and all four had sat still for a good few minutes just trying to take stock and return to normal.

After a while, PC Snap had called for backup and in minutes, Sgt Brown, Lucy, Beth and Archie's mum and what seemed to be most of the circus had descended on the small clearing in the wood.

PC Snap was desperate for some answers. How had Beth and Archie got into the park, how had they got out of the station, let alone how had they managed to get ahead of him and Cynthia and then managed to scale the wall to the park? But all those questions would have to wait for another day. Beth and Archie had had many adventures with PC Snap, but nothing quite as scary and dangerous as this one. Both of them were clearly very shaken by the event and utterly exhausted and now was not the time to start asking too many questions. Their mum gathered them up as only a mummy can do, bundled them into her car and whisked them home. He would talk to them in the morning and give them a polite, yet firm reminder that when he told them to do something, it would always be for a good reason!

PC Snap had tried to have a conversation with Cynthia, but they had only managed to have the briefest of exchanges. PC Snap hadn't really known what to say. He had never been very good in those sort of situations, and it seemed, from the way she had reacted, that neither was Cynthia. The whole event had been a little bit awkward. There were lots of other people around and everyone's focus was on getting the sleeping lion back to the circus and the security of his cage before he woke up. PC Snap had tried to help, but eventually realised that he was just getting in the way, so he took a backwards step and left everyone else to it.

Just before the circus lorry was about to leave, Cynthia burst out of the crowd and ran over towards where PC Snap and Louie were standing, looking slightly out of place. Cynthia gave Louie a big hug and thanked him for saving the day. Then she stretched up, shook PC Snap's hand and thanked him for everything. She turned around and ran a few yards before she stopped suddenly, span around, dashed back and gave him a delicate kiss on his cheek, whispering lightly into his ear, "You're really rather lovely," before once again sprinting off towards the throng of people surrounding the sleeping Paul. PC Snap touched his cheek lightly and wondered if he would ever see Cynthia again?

Sensing that tonight had not been normal, Louie flopped his head on his master's leg and fixed him with a loving stare. They sat for a minute or two before PC Snap patted him on the head. "Thanks mate," he whispered in his ear, before slipping a treat into Louie's warm mouth. "Come on then," he muttered, and the two of them trotted off home.

By the time they arrived home, the birds were singing and it was, to all intents and purposes, morning. PC Snap let himself in to the front door, having glanced up at Beth and Archie's bedroom window. Archie was a little too slow in closing the curtains and, despite his best efforts to quickly close them, he knew PC Snap had seen that he had stayed up to check that he had got home safely before going to bed himself. PC Snap smiled wryly, they would be tired teddies tomorrow.

PC Snap had no idea how his mother did it. Whenever he came home from one of his adventures, there was always a fresh slice of ginger cake and a piping hot cup of cocoa waiting for him, but no sign of his mum.

He devoured both, making sure that Louie had his fair share. The saviour of the night padded off to his bed beside the log fire and was asleep in an instant. PC Snap paused to watch his nose and paws start twitching, a sure sign he was asleep, and wondered whether Louie was chasing rabbits or lions in his dreams.

Climbing the stairs as carefully as he could, PC Snap crept into his room and, as quietly as possible, undressed. He slid into bed and, although almost

instantly falling asleep, he had enough time to remind himself that he had left his truncheon and handcuffs on the floor again. He mustn't forget them when he leapt out of bed in the morning!